Siege

Jacqueline Pearce

Orca currents

OCT 1 8 2014

ORCA BOO

Copyright © 2014 Jacqueline Pearce

Library and Archives Canada Cataloguing in Publication

Pearce, Jacqueline, 1962-, author
Siege / Jacqueline Pearce.
(Orca currents)

Issued in print and electronic formats.
ISBN 978-1-4598-0751-8 (pbk.).—ISBN 978-1-4598-0754-9 (bound).—
ISBN 978-1-4598-0752-5 (pdf).—ISBN 978-1-4598-0753-2 (epub)

I. Title. II. Series: Orca currents
PS8581.E26S53 2014   jc813'.6   C2014-901588-7
                   C2014-901589-5

First published in the United States, 2014
Library of Congress Control Number: 2014935395

Summary: Fourteen-year-old Jason and his friends witness a crime
at a War of 1812 reenactment camp.

*Orca Book Publishers is dedicated to preserving the environment and has
printed this book on Forest Stewardship Council® certified paper.*

Orca Book Publishers gratefully acknowledges the support for its
publishing programs provided by the following agencies: the Government
of Canada through the Canada Book Fund and the Canada Council for the Arts,
and the Province of British Columbia through the BC Arts Council
and the Book Publishing Tax Credit.

Cover photography by Getty Images
Author photo by Danielle Naherniak

ORCA BOOK PUBLISHERS   ORCA BOOK PUBLISHERS
PO Box 5626, Stn. B   PO Box 468
Victoria, BC Canada   Custer, WA USA
v8R 6s4   98240-0468

www.orcabook.com
Printed and bound in Canada.

17 16 15 14 • 4 3 2 1

For my nieces and nephews

Chapter One

Gunfire rings in my ears.

"Second line...Fire!" Major Helston, our commanding officer, yells above the noise.

I squeeze the trigger of my musket and...nothing happens. I try again.

Poof. Gunpowder bursts in my face. A rotten-egg smell stings my nose.

1

"Flash in the pan," my cousin Sean says near my ear. Trust him to know the 1812 name for a gun misfire.

According to the rules for this phony battle, a soldier whose gun doesn't fire is a dead soldier. I glance behind me, hoping Major Helston hasn't noticed my firing fail. But there he is, stepping out of the smoke like a devil in his red British officer's uniform. His rust-colored cheek whiskers flare out like flames on either side of his face.

"Soldier!" He lifts a beefy finger and points right at me. "You're dead!"

I clutch at my chest as if I've been shot and drop to the ground. This is so lame. Sean steps over my body as his line advances. I groan as if I'm not quite dead yet and shift position, trying to trip him. Instead, I snag his foot, and he kicks me in the ribs.

"Serves you right," he says as he marches on without me.

I lie on the field as the rest of my battalion marches forward. Musket smoke rises around me, and I can't see if there's anyone else on the ground. I'm sweating in this hot uniform. There's no shade, and it's got to be ninety degrees out here. The grass under my cheek is dry and prickly, and a rock jabs into my hip. I think an ant is crawling up my pant leg. Why did I let Sean talk me into this?

When Sean invited me camping with him in Canada this summer, reenactment camp was not what I had in mind. His family has an RV, so I thought we'd be at one of those big campgrounds with a swimming pool and miniature golf... and girls. And showers. And Internet access and electricity for recharging my phone. Although it doesn't matter that we have no electricity and no Internet, since Major Hell Storm confiscated all our phones and devices. Because, of course, soldiers in 1812 did not have electronics.

There wasn't much I could do once I got to my aunt and uncle's place in Toronto and found out where Sean planned to drag me. I couldn't turn around and go back to Syracuse. My parents had already left for Switzerland and their big European cruise.

"It'll be fun, Jason," Sean had said. "Like laser tag, but with muskets."

Right. At least with laser tag the guns work. And I've never had to spend the whole game lying on the ground dressed like an idiot and sweating like a pig. Sean didn't mention the War of 1812 soldier uniforms until after his dad dropped us off at Old Fort Erie, and it was too late for me to back out. We don't even get to wear the proper red coats (for the British and Canadian soldiers) or blue coats (for the Americans) until the big battle at the end of the week.

Instead, we've all got baggy white shirts and white pants with suspenders. They call the pants *breeches*, and instead of a zipper, they have a flap with buttons. Kind of like the style pirates wore, I guess. But without the cool factor.

I peer through the smoke, trying to make out the lines of play soldiers. Something bumps my foot. I look up past a pair of black officer's boots and see a long tanned hand reach down through the smoke.

"On your feet, soldier," orders Lieutenant Gunner, our second in command.

Chapter Two

I take Lieutenant Gunner's hand, and he pulls me up in one swift, strong movement. He's tall, lean and way younger than Major Helston. He actually looks good in his tight-fitting red jacket and tall black hat with its shiny plate and white plume. He looks like an officer in a movie about the War of 1812.

"You've recovered," he says. "It's a miracle!"

He grins at me like we're both in on the joke, and I smile back. Could it be that easy? I glance around for Major Helston.

"Don't worry about Helston," Gunner says, as if he's read my mind. "He won't see us until the smoke's cleared, and by then the battle will be over." He nods toward my musket. "So what's the problem?"

I explain about my musket misfiring. He's going to think I'm a real loser. Instead, he nods.

"Pretty common with nineteenth-century muskets," he says. "Make sure you clean it before you load it again." He holds his own gun out to me. "Give this one a try. It's primed and loaded."

I exchange my musket for his and take aim across the field. Through the rising smoke and bright orange blasts of musket fire, I see the white uniforms of the other soldiers. I can't tell which side is which. I hesitate for a second, reminding myself that there are no bullets in the gun. Then I squeeze the trigger.

Bang!

I feel the gun kick back in my hands as flame and smoke burst from the end of the barrel. Cool.

"Reload, soldier," Gunner orders. There is a note of amusement in his voice—like he's not taking this stuff half as seriously as everyone else seems to be.

I grin, thumb open the priming pan and take a paper cartridge from the cartridge box hanging at my side. I bite off the top of the cartridge, tap a bit of powder into the pan and then close the pan. I glance at Gunner to check that I've done it right, and he nods. Then I lower the musket butt to the ground and pour the rest of the powder down the barrel. I raise the gun, get in position and fire.

Bang!

Another perfect fire.

"Well done," says Gunner.

I thank him and hand back the musket.

"Not much point to being here if you don't get to shoot," he says.

After the battle ends, I catch up to Sean outside the mess hall. It's actually a big white tent set up outside the walls of the fort. Our sleeping tents are lined up at this end of the field too. And when I say *field*, I mean it. That's all there is. There's a dry ditch around the fort walls, and then a big, flat grassy area with some trees at one end. No swimming pool. No miniature golf. No junk-food store. No anything.

Sean's face is pink from sun and exertion. I notice his breeches are still white, while mine are stained with dirt and grass. He grins when he sees me.

"That was cool, hey?" he says.

I lift one eyebrow and don't smile. "I wouldn't know. I spent it lying on the ground." For some reason, I don't tell him about Lieutenant Gunner. Maybe I don't want to admit that shooting a musket actually was pretty cool.

Sean's eyes drop to my musket, which I'm kind of leaning on like a crutch, with the muzzle pointed to the sky.

"You're supposed to hold it like this when you're at rest," he says, jiggling the gun on his shoulder. "If that was primed, it could discharge and shoot you in the face."

I scowl at him, and then I remember that I haven't cleaned the gun yet. Quickly, I shift the musket to my shoulder. Sean is *way* too into this. He's lucky he's my favorite cousin.

We leave our muskets propped next to an empty table and join the food line. The food laid out on a long table smells good. But they served us a few weird things last night when we arrived, so my expectations are not high. Behind the table is an older woman and a teenage girl who might be mother and daughter. They're both wearing old-fashioned cloth caps and long dresses with aprons over top. We definitely will not be getting hamburgers or hot dogs.

When I finally get to the table, I grab a plate and hold it up. Ahead of me, the woman serves Sean something that looks like beef stew.

"Cock-a-leekie soup?" asks the girl. She holds a big wooden ladle over a large pot.

"What?" I raise an eyebrow.

She laughs, and I notice she has a dimple in one cheek. Strands of curly black hair escape from under her white cap.

"I know," she says. "Sounds rude, but it's chicken soup." She lifts the lid off the pot, and a delicious smell escapes with the steam.

"Sure," I say. "I'll risk it."

I watch her ladle soup into a bowl. How does a cute girl like her end up in the middle of a bunch of nerds like this?

"So, is this a summer job?" I ask as she hands me the bowl.

"Job?" she echoes. Again, that cute dimple appears in her cheek. "My da's stationed at the fort," she says. "He's in the King's 8th Regiment. Ma and I stay in the barracks with him." She nods toward the older woman.

For a second I wonder if the girl is a few fries short of a Happy Meal, but then I realize she is playing a part. I want to ask her more, but the guy behind me is getting impatient. She gives me a sort of wink as she turns to serve him. At least I think it's a wink. Did I imagine it? She glances back at me, her dark eyes sparkling. Is she flirting with me, or laughing at me?

I move on to the stew and then grab a couple of slices of bread and catch up to Sean. We find the table where we left our muskets and slide onto the bench seat.

Carter and Arman, two guys we met yesterday, sit across from us. They remind me of those Muppets, Bert and Ernie. Carter, the one with the round head like Ernie, has brown hair gelled into short tufts on top of his head. I'm surprised the major didn't confiscate his hair gel when he took our phones and stuff.

"Dude, did you see all that smoke?" says Arman, the one with the long face. He looks like he could be from the Middle East, which doesn't exactly fit the Bert and Ernie comparison. Or the North American War of 1812. But then, I'm part Ukrainian on my mom's side, which doesn't exactly fit either.

"When they fought for real, how did they tell who they were shooting at?" Arman asks.

Carter punches him in the shoulder. "Pretty hard to hit anyone when your gun doesn't fire," he jokes.

"Yeah, yeah," Arman says, punching him back.

I'm relieved to hear that I wasn't the only one with musket trouble. I notice there is a smudge of black down Arman's cheek, which must be the result of the gunpowder flashing in his face. Do I have black on my face too? Is that why the girl was laughing at me?

I glance over at the food table, but the girl isn't there anymore. My eyes rove over the rows of guys in white soldier costumes. Do I look as stupid as they do?

"Hey," says Arman. "You know we're sitting right on a spot where people actually died?"

"So?" says Sean. "There was fighting all over the Niagara area in the War of 1812."

"Yeah, but some of the bloodiest was right here," Arman says. "Over three thousand guys were injured or killed when the British, the Canadian militia and First Nations warriors tried to take the fort back from the Americans."

"Yeah, I know," Sean says. Of course, *he* would.

"Have you heard about the ghosts?" asks Carter.

"Ghosts?" I repeat skeptically.

"Well…" Carter lowers his voice and leans toward us. "There were these two American soldiers camped near the fort. One guy was giving the other one a shave."

"You know, with one of those long sharp razors," Arman adds.

"Then suddenly," continues Carter, "a British cannon ball comes flying in, and *ffttt*—" He swipes his hand past Arman's neck.

"So," Arman finishes, "the dude getting shaved loses his head. The other one loses his hand."

"Jeez!" I groan, half disgusted, half laughing.

"It's true," Sean says. "I heard people have seen a headless ghost and a handless ghost wandering around the fort."

I roll my eyes.

"And they're not the only ghosts," says a voice from behind me. I jump as a water jug smacks down on the table by my elbow.

The guys all laugh. I turn around to see the girl in the old-fashioned cap and dress, a mocking grin on her face.

Chapter Three

It's dark by ten o'clock, which means we're all in our tents attempting to sleep. At home I'd be up for hours yet, watching TV or playing online games with friends. But without electricity, there's not much to do.

I wonder where that girl from the mess hall is now. Is she back home, maybe texting her friends about all the nerdy idiots at reenactment camp? I shift around in my sleeping bag, trying to get comfortable. It's stinking hot, so I unzip the bag and throw it open, knocking off the scratchy old blanket that's meant to hide the sleeping bag and air mattress from passing tourists. I hear the buzz of a mosquito and smile as Sean swears and rustles deeper into his sleeping bag next to me. He is a magnet for mosquitoes. They fly into the tent, sniff the air (or whatever mosquitoes do) and head straight for him.

I sigh with exaggerated contentment as I stretch out my bare arms and rest them behind my head.

"Jerk!" Sean grumbles into his sleeping bag. "I need some bug spray!"

"Not very 1812 of you," I say.

He swears again. I smirk and listen to him thrash around. It's almost completely black inside the tent. I can just make out his lumpy form and darker shadows in the corners where we've piled our stuff. I try to close my eyes, but they pop open. How do they expect us to fall asleep this early? I stare at the dark ceiling, wishing I had my cell phone and could play some games.

"Psst..." A loud whisper comes from outside the tent. "You guys awake?"

"Of course we're awake," I whisper back.

A dark head pokes between the tent flaps.

"Dudes," says Arman, "wanna go ghost hunting?"

I groan. "Are you kidding?"

"What? Are you scared?" says Arman. "You seemed pretty shaken up when we talked about ghosts at dinner."

I bunch up the scratchy blanket and throw it at his head. "I ain't afraid of no ghosts."

"Are they coming, or not?" Carter whispers from behind Arman.

19

Sean sighs loudly.

"Anything's better than being eaten alive by mosquitoes," he grumbles as he climbs out of his sleeping bag.

"There are more mosquitoes out there," I point out.

"Then we'll have to keep moving," says Sean. "Maybe we can break into the office and find some bug spray."

I laugh. "Now you're talking!" If we can get into the office, maybe I can find my phone.

A few minutes later, we're scaling the back wall of the fort—or at least, attempting to. It's taller than it looks.

"Don't grab my head!" Sean complains as I use him as a step ladder.

"Well, hold still!"

He crouches, bracing himself against the stone wall. I lift one foot to his shoulder, and then the other.

"Ouch! Your feet are digging in!" He protests.

"I can't help it," I say. "Try to stand up, so I can reach higher."

We wobble for a moment like a double-decker newborn calf. Then I stretch one hand for the top of the wall and scrabble for a handhold with the other. I shift my feet for better balance.

Sean groans. Then he tips sideways, and we both fall. Sean lands on the grass, and I land on Sean. He swears and pushes me off. I start rolling into the ditch that surrounds the fort, but Carter grabs my arm.

"Shhh!" Arman hisses, coming up beside us. I can just make out his face in the shadows.

"Where've you been?" I snap as I pick myself up off the ground. I hold out my hand to Sean, and he knocks it away.

"While you guys were clowning around," Arman says, "I was doing recon."

"What?"

"Reconnaissance. You know. Looking around."

"So?" I ask. This guy takes way too long to get to the point.

"So, I found a way in." He gestures farther along the wall. "The west sally port is unlocked."

"What?" I ask again.

Arman grins, his teeth pale purple in the dim light that comes from a security light on the other side of the battlefield. "The back door is open."

Chapter Four

The four of us huddle in the dark shadow of the sally port, looking into the middle of the fort. In front of us, the parade ground is empty. The fort's two-story stone buildings are on the other side of the parade ground. On the left is the building that holds the officers' kitchen, surgery and upstairs museum. On the right, an identical building houses the soldiers' barracks, officers' quarters and officers' mess. The campers' modern stuff is locked in an office on the main floor of the second building. There are no lights in any of the windows and no sign of any guards. The main gate, which is in the center of a tall stone wall between the buildings, is closed.

"Look!" Arman whispers, pointing to a raised corner of the fort to the left of the buildings. "Something moved up on the bastion!"

I squint, trying to make out shapes in the darkness. Above us, a cloud moves free from the half moon, and the fort lightens a notch.

"There's nothing there," I say. But just as I get the words out, a dark lump moves above the edge of the wall. A head?

We jerk back into the sally port.

"Ouch! Watch it!" Carter whispers as Arman steps on his feet.

24

"Shhh!" Sean hisses. The sound echoes against the stone walls of the sally port like someone we can't see is shushing back at us. Sean grabs my arm and whispers low in my ear. "We shouldn't be in here. This was a stupid idea."

Cautiously, I poke my head out from the door and look up to the corner again.

"Is it the ghost of the headless soldier?" Arman asks. He's joking, but his voice has gone up a pitch.

I pull back into the doorway. "No," I say. "Whoever it is definitely has a head. I didn't see any hands though."

Arman laughs, but it sounds forced. The laugh echoes against the walls.

"Shhh!" Sean hisses again. And again, the sound echoes. This time it sounds like a snake is hiding between the stones. I feel the hairs prickle at the back of my neck.

"So," says a hushed voice just outside the doorway. "What are you brave soldiers up to tonight?"

I almost jump out of my skin before I recognize the voice. It's the girl from the mess tent. She steps out of the shadows, and I see that she is still wearing her old-fashioned dress. Her eyes are bright in the moonlight, and the dimple is a tiny shadow on her cheek. She twitches the skirt of the dress as if trying to shift it over her feet. Is she wearing flip-flops?

"Just getting a breath of fresh air," Sean says. He steps forward as if he is our leader and wasn't being a wuss a minute ago. I fight the urge to shove him into the wall.

"I'm Nicola, by the way," the girl says. We introduce ourselves, still talking in whispers.

"We're looking for ghosts," Arman volunteers. I groan. Can't this guy keep his mouth shut?

now close enough to the bastion
can hear a hushed voice. I can
ramp that goes up to the bastion,
n't see what's at the top. If the
up there decides to leave, he will
lown the ramp and walk right
What happens if we get caught?
Helston kick me out of camp?
cola from her job? Earlier today
n't have minded getting kicked
camp. But now I'm starting to
might want to stick around and
it goes.

la slips past me. "Come on," she
s, her breath warm on my ear.
reep up the ramp and crouch in
ows. I look back across the fort
the sally port entrance. I can't
an and the others are still there.
an hear the voice clearly now,
ow and slightly distorted. I can't
t who it is. I glance at Nicola,
shrugs.

"Oh yeah?" Nicola asks. The dimple is still in her cheek, and I'm pretty sure she's silently laughing at us.

"You realize you're standing in the middle of the ghost hot spot?" she says.

We all do a quick three-sixty.

"Are you serious?" asks Arman.

"Of course," says Nicola. "I'm always serious."

"Oh yeah?" I say skeptically.

She flashes me a quick grin, and then her face goes deadpan. "Yeah. At least fourteen people working in the fort quit after they saw something in this sally port."

"Like what?" I ask.

She shrugs. "Something that scared them."

"The headless ghost?" Carter asks.

She shrugs again. "Maybe."

Arman swears.

"Shut up," Sean says. "She's playing you."

"Quiet!" I gesture for everyone to step back into the sally port. There's definitely something moving up on that bastion.

Nicola steps closer to me, and we peer around the corner. There's a dim light up by the top of the wall, and it's moving. A ghost lantern?

"I wonder who that is," Nicola whispers. "It looks like they're talking on a cell phone."

Of course. That's what the light is. I can't believe I was starting to think like Arman. Either someone else from the camp broke into the office and liberated a cell phone, or our commanding officer is not following his own rules.

"It could be Major Hell Storm," I whisper close to Nicola's ear. Her hair smells like peaches.

She pauses, and despite the darkness, I see her mouth quirk to one side.

"It's not him," she says. "He's in the office."

"Right," says the voice. "Saturday it is."

There is a tiny beep as the phone conversation ends, and then the crunch of feet moving toward us.

Nicola gives me a frantic shove, and we scramble back down the ramp. The building with the officers' kitchen and the surgery is on our left. The door to the kitchen is only a few steps away. Do we have time to get to it? Will it be unlocked?

The footsteps stop as the guy pauses at the top of the ramp. Nicola reaches her hand out to the kitchen doorknob. The door opens, but instead of stepping inside, she closes the door again with a bang and turns to me.

"Pretty spooky, hey?" she says, no longer whispering. My heart thumps. What is she doing?

"Half the kitchen was destroyed when the gunpowder magazine blew up," she continues, as if she's giving a tour and we've just come out of the kitchen. "A lot of soldiers died there."

I look over my shoulder toward the bastion. A dark figure closes in on us.

Chapter Five

"What are you two doing here?" It's Lieutenant Gunner. As he approaches, I see that he's taken off his uniform jacket and hat but is still wearing the shirt and breeches.

"I'm giving Jason the ghost tour," Nicola tells him.

"Oh yeah?" he looks from Nicola to me and grins. I let out a relieved breath.

I notice the shape of the cell phone still in his hand (no pockets in these breeches). Gunner seems to notice where I'm looking.

"I had to check in with the girl-friend," he says, holding up the cell phone in a you-caught-me gesture. He smiles. "You know how it is."

I grin back at him. Figures. He must have been making plans to meet with her Saturday night.

The three of us walk toward the main gate. My eyes flick across the courtyard to the sally port. I think I see a shadow move and maybe a hand wave. Is it Sean? I'm thinking I better say goodbye to Nicola and head back to camp, when a voice booms across the courtyard.

"What's going on here?"

We all freeze as Major Helston steps out of the shadows.

"The inside of the fort is off-limits for campers after dark," Helston says.

I notice he used the word *campers* instead of *soldiers*. A slip? "Who gave you permission to be here?" he demands, glaring directly at me.

Before I can think of what to say, Lieutenant Gunner steps forward.

"I did, sir." He turns to me. "Jason, isn't it?"

I nod, and Gunner continues. "Jason was helping me after the battle, and I told him Nicola and I would give him a night tour."

I give an inward sigh of relief. Lieutenant Gunner is all right.

"I see," Helston says, his glare taking in Nicola and Gunner. "I'd appreciate it if you'd check with me next time. I need to know that people are where they're supposed to be," he adds, with a pointed look at Gunner. "We don't want anyone wandering around in the dark and falling into the dry ditch."

"Sorry, Dad," Nicola says. "I'll give him the rest of the tour tomorrow."

Did she just say *Dad*?

"Well, I'm off to bed," she says. "Good night!" She smiles and waves as if getting caught by her dad in a dark fort with two guys in the middle of the night is no big deal.

Helston huffs, like he wants to say more. I figure this is a good time for me to get out of there. I start toward the sally port.

"Where do you think you're going?!" Helston bellows.

"Um…back to camp," I mumble.

"Lieutenant Gunner," Helston orders. "See that this soldier gets back to his tent safely." He jerks his head toward the main gate. "That way."

When I arrive at the tent, Sean is already inside. Arman and Carter must already be back at their tent as well.

"That was a close one," Sean whispers. He sounds slightly out of breath. He and the other guys must have made pretty good time getting back to camp the back way.

It's not until I'm inside my sleeping bag again that I remember my phone still sitting in the office.

Chapter Six

The next morning, I stand on the field next to Sean, musket raised to my shoulder. Major Helston strides in front of us, wearing his red jacket and tall black officer's hat. He looks imposing as he surveys the line of phony soldiers. His gaze falls on me, and he pauses. His bushy orange eyebrows knit together and his cheek whiskers bristle. I pull my shoulders back and straighten up. The day is hot already, and I feel sweat start to drip under my arms. Helston moves on, and I relax slightly. Weird. Why am I letting him get under my skin when this is all playacting? Did the real soldiers squirm like this when their commanding officer looked at them? Of course, if they'd done anything wrong, they could be whipped. Or forced to listen to bagpipe music, or something. All I have to worry about is getting kicked out of camp.

"On June 19, 1812, the United States declared war on Britain. This meant the United States was at war with Canada, which was a British colony," Helston says, his voice booming out over the field. "Can anyone tell me why?"

Of course Sean speaks up. "Britain was disrupting shipping off the US coast. They wanted to stop the United States from trading with France," he calls out.

"And they were forcing US sailors to join the British navy."

"That's right," Helston says, with a nod at Sean. "The British Empire was the superpower back then. Britain was at war with France, and they didn't like the US sending supplies to their enemy. The British navy needed more sailors, and they figured some of those American sailors were still British enough to join...Anything else?"

Beside me, Sean shifts slightly. I nudge him in the ribs before he can open his mouth.

"What?" he whispers.

"Stop sucking up to Hell Storm," I whisper back. "Give someone else a chance to answer."

Sean scowls.

"Indians," someone else calls out. Helston stops pacing and stops in front of Arman.

"Who?" He pins Arman with his stare.

"Um," Arman mumbles. I'm sure he regrets attracting Helston's attention.

"Speak up," Helston orders.

"The First Nations," Arman says. Helston frowns, but Arman goes on. "The United States wanted more of their land, and the British were giving the First Nations dudes guns to help them stop the US."

Helston nods and begins pacing again. If he's not careful, he's going to wear a path in the grass.

"That's right," he says. "The Iroquois, Shawnee and other tribes wanted to keep their lands, and the British wanted to keep control of the northern fur trade. They were willing to work together to stop the United States from expanding."

He stops and glares like he'll turn the firing squad on us if we don't pay attention. I try to look interested, but I'm dying to get off this hot field and into someplace with air-conditioning. My musket feels like it's getting heavier.

"When the American army marched into Upper Canada," Helston continues, "they thought it would be a cake walk. They thought the settlers up here would be happy to join them in throwing out the British. Lots of people had family and friends on both sides of the border and didn't want to fight. But when US soldiers attacked their homes and farms and burned the towns of Newark and York, do you think the settlers felt like siding with the Americans?"

"York is Toronto," Sean whispers to me. "Newark is Niagara-on-the-Lake."

"I know," I snap back. Although I didn't.

"No!" Helston finishes his own question, pounding his right fist into his left hand. "They got mad."

His gaze roves over us. "What did they do to retaliate?"

"March on Washington and burn the White House!" Sean calls out.

Really? There is a murmur along the line of pseudo soldiers. I guess I'm not the only one that didn't know the White House got attacked.

"That's right," Helston says with a chilling smile. "Before the war, Americans sat down to supper in Canadian houses. Canadians crossed the Niagara River to visit their American cousins. During the war, they were burning each other's capitals. The Americans thought the British Canadians would be pushovers. They got a surprise. The British thought their navy ruled the world. They also got a surprise when they faced the new US navy."

"Now," Helston says, turning to survey us again. "Today we're going to do a little reenactment inside the fort."

I groan, picturing more time spent lying on the ground. Beside me, Sean looks ready to burst with eagerness.

Helston divides us into British and US troops. This time Sean is on the British side, and I'm on the American. The British guys march into the fort with Helston. The rest of us hike down to the river with Lieutenant Gunner. He's wearing a blue uniform jacket now instead of a red one.

We stand in the shade by some trees. The river is wide and flat. It's hard to tell there is a current until a stick floats by. Across the river is the city of Buffalo, New York. Modern buildings, cars, video games, air-conditioning, people who live in the twenty-first century. If I walked out of this camp, it wouldn't take that long to get to the Peace Bridge and cross over to Buffalo. I could probably even swim across from here.

"If any of you are thinking of going for a swim," Gunner says, as if he's read my mind, "you'd better be good swimmers. That current is stronger than it looks, and twenty-seven kilometers east, it drops over Niagara Falls."

So much for my escape plan. I've seen Niagara Falls, and I'm not taking any chances.

"The Americans first attacked this fort in May 1813," Gunner tells us. "The British surrendered, and the Americans occupied the fort for a while. Then, in December 1813, the American troops in this whole area got pushed back across the river. They burned a few places before they left, leaving a lot of people homeless right at the start of winter." He pauses to let this sink in.

"Then, of course, the British army and the Canadian militia retaliated by burning places on US soil—including Washington and Buffalo." He waves back across the river. There is an edge of boredom in his voice. Like he's told this story too many times.

"The Americans attacked again on July 3, 1814," Gunner continues. He grins, the enthusiasm back in his voice. "And that's the battle we're doing today, boys," he says, holding up his musket.

I look across the field at the low stone walls of the fort. I see some heads peering over the top of the bastions at the corners of the fort. But mostly the soldiers are hidden, their musket barrels pointing out through slits along the top of the stone walls. One cannon faces us on a grass-covered mound that partly blocks our view of the fort. More cannons aim out from the side walls.

Down by the river, we spread out in a line and load our muskets. The guy next to me nudges me with his elbow.

"Don't forget your earplugs," he whispers, just before Lieutenant Gunner's voice rings out.

"Forward march!"

Chapter Seven

We march toward the fort and then stop.

"Make ready!" Gunner commands. We raise our guns.

"Present!" We point them at the fort.

"Fire!"

I squeeze the trigger, half expecting the musket to blow up in my face. Instead, flame and smoke burst from the barrel.

Muskets blast on either side of me, and I'm glad of the earplugs.

"In the heat of a real battle you'd be listening for whistle signals through the noise," Gunner tells us. His voice is barely audible above all the noise. "The Americans used whistles, the British used drums," he adds.

We continue forward. I fire again and again. Smoke, yells and the smell of gunpowder rise around me. I feel a surge of adrenaline. As we get closer to the fort, I make out Sean's pale face above the bastion wall. I aim my musket at him and, for a second, wonder what it would feel like to fire real bullets (or musket balls). Like Helston said, some guys would have been firing at their own cousins in this war. It's weird to imagine. What would I have done if I was a real soldier back then and I recognized someone I was shooting at? My finger hesitates on the trigger as I consider this. Before I come up with an answer, the fort's front gate opens. A hand reaches out, waving a white cloth. They've surrendered.

Everyone on the field cheers.

"Wasn't that too easy?" I ask Gunner, who is nearby. It seems to me the guys in the fort should have been able to pick us off easily as we marched across the open ground.

"Yeah, in this battle, the British gave up without much of a fight," says Gunner. "The commander was actually court-martialed for surrendering too quickly. But the British made up for it when they tried to get the fort back. That siege lasted almost two months. By the time it ended, three thousand five hundred men were injured, dead or missing."

"Wow," I say, looking back at the field we just marched across. I try to picture it littered with real bodies. Real people.

"Fort Erie reenacts the main battles every year," Gunner tells me. "You guys get to be part of that this Saturday."

The fort's gates open wide, and we march inside. I help Gunner and a few of the other guys hoist an old-fashioned American flag up the flagpole. Major Helston announces that we have a half-hour break before lunch, and I decide to look for Sean. I hate to admit it, but the morning wasn't as boring as I thought it would be.

I walk past the officers' kitchen toward the east bastion, where I had seen Sean during the battle. When I reach the ramp, I hear a voice that sounds like his.

"The fireworks will be cool."

Fireworks? I hurry to the top of the ramp and round the corner. Sure enough, Sean is leaning against the stone wall. I jerk to a stop. Standing next to him is Nicola. No one else is up here.

"Hey," Nicola says when she sees me. "Congratulations on the big victory." Her cheek has that teasing dimple again.

"'Sup?" Sean nods at me. Is he trying to sound cool? "Did you hear we get to have fireworks Saturday night?" He sounds like his nerdy self again. "The battle is going to be epic!"

"You know," says Nicola, "the big explosion happened right here—when the British tried to get the fort back from the Americans on the night of August 15, 1814."

"Yeah, I know. Right here at the fort," says Sean.

"No, I mean right where we're standing," says Nicola. "The British came over the wall and took this bastion. The American artillery retreated into that part of the fort." She points toward the parade ground. "There was a big gunfight right inside the fort. Then the

Americans turned the cannon on the back wall around to face the bastion." She gestures to the wall beside the sally port where we snuck in last night. "And the British turned the cannon on the bastion around, so they could shoot back."

"That's close range to be firing cannons," says Sean.

"Yeah," says Nicola. "Not only that. The cannon here was right on top of the spot where all the fort's gunpowder was stored. It was hit by a spark, and the whole thing blew up. It took out this whole end of the building and all the British soldiers who'd just come over the wall. There were bodies everywhere."

Both Sean and I look around the bastion as if we expect to see the bodies. My eyes drop to the ground under my feet. I know the explosion happened two hundred years ago, but it's creepy to be standing right at the spot.

"There's no gunpowder under there now, right?" Sean asks.

"Actually," says Nicola, "the gunpowder for the camp's muskets and the fireworks is in a storage room right there." She points to the ground between us and the building wall.

"Oh!" I say, making an exaggerated move for the ramp, as if another explosion could happen any minute.

Nicola laughs and grabs my arm. I pretend that I want to get away, making her hold on to me longer. Sean gives me a dirty look and turns away, and I can't help smiling.

"Look down there," Sean says. I'm pretty sure he's just trying to interrupt my moment with Nicola.

"What is it?" Nicola asks. She drops my arm to go look over the wall. She has to stand on her toes to see over the top.

"Down by the river," Sean says. He leans in closer to Nicola and points. When she doesn't move away, he looks over his shoulder at me and grins. I glare at him and move to Nicola's other side.

I look down over the field we just marched across, following the direction Sean is pointing. At the river's edge below the fort, two long open boats sit on the beach. They look old-fashioned, so I guess they belong to the fort. Someone is down there, walking around the boats.

"Is that Major Helston?" Sean asks. The guy is wearing a white shirt and what looks like white breeches and tall black boots.

"I can't tell. Maybe it's Lieutenant Gunner."

"What's he doing?"

"Probably checking the boats before you guys take them out on the river," says Nicola.

"Cool!" Sean says. "When do we get to do that?"

"Tomorrow, I think."

I look out at the river, remembering what Gunner said about the current flowing to Niagara Falls.

"Are you sure it's safe?" I ask.

"You're not scared, are you?" Sean asks. Like he's the brave one.

"You'll be fine," Nicola says, bumping her shoulder against my arm. "You know how to row, don't you?"

I shrug.

"Look at all those boats out there." She waves a hand toward the river, which is dotted with modern recreational boats. She shields her eyes from the sun. "It's perfectly safe if you know what you're doing."

"That's my point," I say. "Do you trust any of us with a boat?"

With perfect timing, Arman and Carter appear at the top of the bastion ramp, and I make a sweeping gesture that takes in Sean, the two of them and me. Nicola laughs.

"What?" Arman demands as he and Carter join us.

We explain about the boats. Arman admits he's never picked up an oar or paddle of any kind, but Carter and Sean claim some skill.

"There, you see?" Nicola says.

"Now there's a boat I wouldn't mind taking for a ride," Carter says, pointing to a sleek modern speedboat cruising up the river.

"That's the border patrol," says Nicola.

"Really?" The sun glares off the water, and I squint to make out the details of the gray boat. "Are they looking for people crossing the border illegally?"

"That and smugglers," she says.

"Smugglers?" Sean asks.

"Yeah, people have been smuggling stuff across this river since before the War of 1812," Nicola explains. "Slaves used to cross here to get to freedom. In the 1920s and '30s, when it was illegal to sell alcohol in the states, rum-running was a big deal. Nowadays people smuggle cigarettes, drugs, people... even cheese."

I laugh.

"You're kidding," says Carter. "People smuggle cheese?"

"Well, I wouldn't call it a major criminal operation, but it's been done," says Nicola.

"Don't small boats go back and forth here all the time?" Sean asks. "It seems like it would be easy to drop off a person or a package without being noticed. I bet you could even swim across."

"It's not as easy as it looks," Nicola says. "The water is shallow here, which makes the current fast, and the border patrol keeps watch—especially since 9/11. But people still try."

As we talk, the boat picks up speed. Its bow lifts out of the water, and white water sprays out behind the two big motors at the back of the boat.

"I wonder if they're after someone now," Arman says.

As the boat speeds upriver, the growl of its engines reaches us on the walls of the fort. It doesn't seem to be chasing anyone. My eyes drift back to the two old-fashioned boats on the shore. The guy down there is gone now.

"Come on, boys," Nicola says. "Let's go for lunch."

Chapter Eight

It feels cooler in the shade of the mess tent when we first get there, but by the time we finish eating, it's like a sauna. Every inch of me is dripping sweat. I'm tempted to sneak off and jump in the river. The current can't be that strong if they're going to let us take row boats out on it.

"Hey." I lean in close to whisper my suggestion to Sean, but I'm cut off when Lieutenant Gunner calls for our attention.

He stands at the head of the tent with a large sack on the ground beside him.

"I have a surprise for you," he says with a grin. Then he pauses and glances around as if checking that he's not being watched. The rest of us look around too, wondering what he's up to. There is no sign of Major Helston, and I don't see Nicola or her mom either. The idea that Gunner might be about to show us something that Hell Storm wouldn't like has us interested.

Gunner reaches into the sack and lifts out a gun. Not a musket. Not anything from 1812. This gun is yellow, orange and green plastic. A Super Soaker water gun. He dumps the whole sack on the table next to him, and out pours the biggest pile of water guns I've ever seen.

"Gentlemen, choose your weapon."

We jump from our benches and rush for the guns.

By the time darkness settles and we climb into our sleeping bags that night, I'm exhausted. It's still stinking hot, so I leave my bag open and lie on top of it.

Sean managed to scrounge some toxic-smelling bug spray earlier. He sprays one last blast of it and then zips his sleeping bag up to his chin despite the heat.

"That was the best day," he says.

"Yeah," I agree. "I wonder what Hell Storm would have made us do if he hadn't taken the afternoon off."

"You think he wouldn't have let us have the water fight?"

"Are you kidding? He'd never let anything plastic into camp."

"You don't like him, do you?" Sean says. I can hear him shift in his sleeping bag, like he's rolled to face me—even though it's black as oil in here.

"And you do?"

"He's not that bad," Sean says with a yawn.

"Yeah, right," I say sarcastically. "Let's just say I'd rather fight on Lieutenant Gunner's team."

"Unit," Sean corrects me, but without much energy.

It's too early and too hot to sleep. But I can already hear Sean's breathing grow slower and deeper. I feel like kicking his sleeping bag, but I can't move. It looks like it will be an exciting night of lying awake, listening to him breathe. That's the last thought I have before I'm dead asleep.

It's still dark in the tent when I wake up. I have no idea what time it is, but I have to pee. I fumble my way out of the tent and stand for a moment, getting my bearings. The rows of silent tents look eerie. From where I stand, the security light is hidden by a tree. The light that falls across the tent roofs looks like moonlight. This must have been what the camp of soldiers looked like two hundred years ago. Maybe I should stay authentic and use a tree instead of a stinking port-a-potty.

I walk past the tents toward the trees. Nothing moves. If this was 1812, soldiers would be keeping watch. Also, all the nearby trees would have been cut down for firewood, or spikes for the dry ditch, or maybe a palisade to protect the soldiers camped outside the fort. When the Americans held the fort in 1814, there would have been over 3,500 soldiers camped here.

I am starting to sound like Sean. I look away from the camp to the modern lights of Buffalo on the other side of the river. I picture people out at restaurants and movies, home watching TV or playing video games. I squint, and the lights blur. I can almost imagine soldiers' campfires dotting the shore. Then, the lights of a boat catch my eye, and I'm back in the present, wondering what has gotten into me. The boat is moving fast. Border patrol? Or maybe it's a smuggler about to make a drop.

My eyes move from the river to the black walls of the fort. There is a flicker of light on top of the wall. Lieutenant Gunner with his cell phone again? But the light isn't clear white like a cell-phone screen. It's yellow and wavers like a candle or a lantern. Maybe it's Major Helston on some kind of midnight watch. He probably doesn't use a flashlight. That would be too modern for him.

The light moves back and forth as if signaling someone or searching for something. Like a lost head? Now I see the shadowy shape of a person holding the lantern. I can make out the guy's arm and his shoulders…And where his head should be—nothing.

Forget the trees and 1812. I run for the stinking, plastic, modern port-a-potties and the bright glow of the security light.

Chapter Nine

"Any of you city slickers know how to row a boat?" Lieutenant Gunner asks.

It's the next day. We've just dragged the two old wooden boats half into the water. In the bright summer light, I'm sure I totally imagined the headless guy on the wall last night. The shadows must have played tricks on me.

"I can row," Sean volunteers.

"Real reenactors don't wear life jackets either," he tells me. "They want to look authentic, so they keep the life jackets hidden in canvas bags under here." He pats the bench.

"Good thing we're not real reenactors," I say. Proper reenactors would be loaded down with heavy coats, muskets and gear. If they fell overboard, they'd sink like cannon balls—just like the real soldiers must have done.

On shore, Major Helston joins Gunner behind our boat. Both of them are wearing their red uniform jackets and black hats (which I now know are called *shakos*). I can see sweat running down Helston's face, but Gunner looks cool. They take hold of the back of the boat and push it toward the water. My heart jumps. They're not going to let us go out on our own, are they? But as soon as the boat slides free of the gravel, Gunner jumps into the back, and we're off.

Right away, I feel the current grab the boat and start pulling us downstream. Sean, Carter and the other oarsmen dig the oars into the water, and we gain control. We head toward the other side of the river and Buffalo. Behind us, the second boat follows, with Major Helston at the stern.

The sun glints off the water, and there's a cool breeze. Major Helston yells something from the boat behind us, interrupting my thoughts. I turn to see him pointing upriver. Gunner waves at him then turns back to us.

"I'm supposed to tell you about the *Ohio*, the *Somers* and the *Porcupine*," he says.

Arman, who isn't rowing, raises his eyebrows. "Sounds like a bunch of cartoon animals."

Carter laughs, and one of his oars catches, splashing Sean.

Gunner shakes his head. "The *Ohio*, the *Somers* and the *Porcupine* were three American armed schooners anchored near the head of the Niagara River, protecting Fort Erie." He gestures downriver in the direction the border patrol boat sped off yesterday.

"When the British army, the Canadian militia and their First Nations allies started setting up siege lines outside the fort, the schooners fired at them from the river. So the British navy carried six small boats overland and put them in the river near here. They disguised them as supply boats and snuck up on the schooners." Gunner pauses while Carter and Sean knock oars and splash the guys sitting ahead of them. We wouldn't be able to sneak up on anyone.

Gunner tips his shako forward to shield his eyes and sighs. "Well, they snuck up in plain sight," he says. "The ships thought they were supply boats. When the British got close, they whipped out their swords and boarded the first two ships. The *Porcupine* cut anchor and ran."

While Gunner talks, I look back at him and the guys rowing. Now Gunner calls to me. "Hey, head man! How's it look up ahead?"

I remember I'm supposed to watch where we're going. I turn around quickly, hoping we're not on a collision course with a speedboat. The river is clear ahead of us. I look to the US shore, expecting to see Buffalo getting closer. But instead, it's almost as far away as when we started. With one difference. It's moving south, and we're moving north. The current is taking us toward Niagara Falls!

Chapter Ten

"Hey!" I twist back to Gunner, trying not to panic. "The current is taking us downriver!"

"Yeah," Gunner says, laughing. "Not so easy to cross, is it?"

"What do we do?" Arman screeches, jumping to his feet. The boat rocks.

"Sit down," Gunner orders. "It's

under control. We'll go with the current and pull up near the bridge."

For the first time, I notice that Gunner is holding on to something at the back of the boat. With relief, I realize it's a rudder, and he's steering the boat. I peer ahead at the arches of the distant bridge. We're closing in on it pretty fast. And there is a speedboat heading directly for us. I call out a warning, and Gunner adjusts the rudder. The oncoming boat sees us at the same time and slows down, veering around us. It growls past. Then its wake rocks us.

"Whoa!" Arman calls out as he grips the side of the boat.

I notice that the Canadian side of the river is getting closer again. Gunner must be steering us toward shore. I see a boat ramp. Some old men and kids are fishing from the rocks nearby. A woman and a girl, both with black curly hair, wave at us from near the ramp. It's Nicola and her mom.

As we near the shore, I wonder if I'm supposed to call back some kind of directions. There's no dock, just a cement ramp between the rocks. What am I supposed to say? A little more to the left? Whose left? Sean and the others are facing one way, and I'm facing another. Am I supposed to say something like *hard to port*? Which side of the boat is port?

I wave at Nicola as if everything is under control then look back at the guys pulling the oars. I feel as useless as one of those wooden figureheads on the front of an old ship. Or worse, a dog wagging his tail and pointing his nose at the shore.

I shift closer to Sean. His face is pink, and he's sweating under his straw hat.

"Hey," I nudge him. "Do you want to trade spots?"

"No," he grunts, gripping the end of the long oar.

"Why not? You look like you could use a break."

"You're supposed to be directing us in," Sean says, breathing hard.

Why is he such a rule-lover?

"Come on. Just give me a turn." I reach for the oar.

"Get lost!" He tries to knock my hand away without letting go of the oar. The paddle catches in the water and splashes.

"Watch it!" Carter says as his oar bumps against Sean's.

The boat rocks.

"Let go!" Sean growls, his face reddening. "Why do you always have to be such a jerk?"

He lifts one hand from the oar to give me a push. I'm not expecting it. I lose my balance. I grab for the side of the boat, but my hand slips on the wet wood. My hip bangs against the edge. The boat rocks again.

"Sit down!" Gunner yells. Too late.

I flip over the side and into the river. Before I can take a breath, cold water closes over my head. Water fills my eyes, and I can't see. For a second, I don't know which way is up or down. Panic spikes through me. But then the life jacket pops me back up to the surface.

I cough up water. Where is the boat? I twist around, flailing my arms. *Stop panicking, you idiot. The shore is close, and you know how to swim.* I try to kick my legs, but my shoes are like weights on the ends of my feet. And the current pulls me down the river.

Great. I'm not going to drown now. I'm just going to float down the river and go over Niagara Falls. And then die.

Someone is yelling my name. Now, the boat is beside me.

"Grab hold!" Sean calls, holding out one of the long oars.

I stretch my hand toward it, trying to kick closer. My fingers touch the oar. Then slide past as the current pulls me away.

"Over here!" another voice calls. Nicola? "Try standing," she says. Does she think I can walk on water?

I turn toward her voice and see rocks and bushes. I'm closer to shore than I realized. I splash my arms, trying to move toward the rocks, but the current is too strong. It's going to pull me right past.

One of my feet hits something. I feel a tug on the back of my life jacket. I jerk sideways, banging my knee on a rock. Someone is pulling me out of the water.

"Thanks!" I gasp, as I collapse on the rock like a beached fish. I look up into the face of an old guy who must be one of the fishermen I saw on the rocks earlier. Beside him, Nicola stares down at me.

Chapter Eleven

"You didn't have to laugh so hard," I complain to Nicola as we begin the long walk back to camp.

"I didn't laugh until I knew you were okay," she says.

By this time, the two boats have been loaded onto a trailer. Nicola's mom and Major Helston are driving back to the fort in the truck, pulling the boats (I still have trouble thinking of Major Helston as Nicola's dad). The rest of us have to walk. They offered to give me a spot in the truck, but that seemed more humiliating than walking back with everyone else.

The sidewalk follows alongside the river through a long narrow park. Sean, Nicola and I are a bit behind the rest of the group.

"You did look pretty funny," Sean says. He flaps his arms in imitation of me floundering in the water. I don't laugh.

"I could have drowned!" I snap.

"The water wasn't even over your head," Sean points out.

"I'd like to see *you* try fighting that current with all *your* clothes on!"

Nicola must sense that I'm ready to hit Sean. She steps in between us.

"Well, I'm glad we didn't lose you," she says, linking her arm through mine.

My anger eases, and I can't resist smiling when I see Sean's gaze drop to

Nicola's arm touching mine. But then she reaches out to take Sean's arm with her free one, and I stop smiling.

We walk in silence for a while. The tension between Sean and me simmers. In the background, we can hear the hum of traffic crossing the Peace Bridge and the drone of boat motors on the river. Gulls screech overhead, and a shard of laughter breaks loose from the group ahead of us. But still, the world seems quiet, except for one sound—the *squelch squelch* of my wet shoes.

Suddenly, the three of us start laughing. We try to stop, but then I take another step. *Squelch*. Our eyes meet, and we burst out laughing again. Now, I picture myself splashing around in the river, and I can see how funny it must have looked. At least, now that I'm safely on shore.

Arman and Carter drop back to join us.

"Look," Arman says, pointing at the river.

The border patrol boat is back. It cruises past, close enough for us to see two uniformed patrol guys on board. One looks through binoculars. He scans the river first and then turns them toward us. For a second, I feel guilty—as if I'm doing something wrong.

"What are they looking for?" Carter asks.

Arman waves.

"Dude," Carter warns. "Don't get their attention."

"Why not?" Arman says. "We're not drug smugglers."

On the water, the boat seems to pause for a second, defying the current. The officer raises a hand in a brief return wave.

Arman laughs. He and Carter high-five like they've achieved some kind of victory.

"See," Nicola says. "They can tell we're harmless."

Yeah, they can tell we're idiots.

It takes us longer than we expected to walk back to the fort. The two boats are already stowed near the spot where we launched them earlier. We follow the other campers up the path to the fort. They don't look much like 1812 soldiers anymore—if they ever did. Everybody drags their feet, and several guys have their shirts off and wrapped around the top of their heads. The breeze through my wet clothes kept me cool most of the walk. But now, my clothes are almost dry, and I feel the heat as we move away from the river.

Most of the guys turn off the path to walk around the fort to the field where we're camped. Sean and I pause to say goodbye to Nicola at the fort's main gate.

A movement on top of the left bastion catches my eye. I look up to see Major Helston standing there peering over the wall. He's not looking down at us but out toward the river. I follow his gaze. The border patrol boat is there again. It's cruising back upriver, and I can swear Hell Storm is watching it, frowning.

Sean and I make plans to meet up with Nicola after dinner, and then we follow the other guys to the campsite.

"What do you think Hell Storm is up to?" I ask Sean as we walk across the grass.

"What are you talking about?" he says.

"You saw the way he was watching the patrol boat," I tell him. "Like he was worried about something."

"You mean like he doesn't want the border patrol to discover his illegal plot?" Sean says sarcastically.

"Exactly," I say.

"You're crazy," Sean says.

"What about yesterday afternoon when he disappeared?" I point out. I'm not serious, but sometimes Sean is fun to mess with.

"He probably had to go into town for something."

"Like what?" I ask.

"I don't know. Maybe he just wanted to get out of the way, so we could have the water-gun fight," Sean suggests. "If he stuck around, he'd have to stay in character and not let us have the plastic guns."

"You mean he got out of the way so we could have some fun?" I say. "Not likely."

"Sometimes you're an idiot," Sean says. "Just because you don't like him doesn't mean he's a bad guy."

Maybe Sean is right. Helston *is* Nicola's dad, so he can't be all bad. Still, I can't help looking over my shoulder up at the bastion. But Helston is gone.

Chapter Twelve

Friday afternoon, the real War of 1812 reenactors start to arrive. The field outside the fort is now divided into three camps. One for us, one for the American soldiers and one for the British soldiers and the rest of the Canadian side. Already, there are rows of new tents set up. They look like an assembly line of white triangles. A larger tent at one end of the Canadian section flies a battered Union Jack flag. An American flag, which is several stars and stripes short, waves from the American camp. Like the British flag, it looks like it's been in the middle of a battle or two. I wonder if the flags are like those jeans you buy with holes already in them, or if they've actually seen some action. Or maybe I should say *reenaction*.

After our afternoon drill, Sean, Arman, Carter and I wander over to the British-Canadian camp. Two middle-aged men in red uniform jackets sit on folding chairs in front of one of the tents. An old-fashioned lantern hangs from a metal stand, and two muskets lean against another stand. It looks like a musket teepee. I notice that their muskets have bayonets attached to the ends of the barrels. The blades look sharp. It's a good thing Major Helston hasn't let us use bayonets on our muskets, or half of us would be in the hospital by now.

The first man has a thick gray moustache and is drinking something from a tin mug. The second man has a long wooden pipe in his mouth, but it doesn't look lit.

"Good afternoon, gentlemen," the moustache man says. The guy with the pipe nods at us.

We stop and say hi. I notice there's straw around the bottom of their tent.

"What's that for?" I ask.

"To keep out drafts and rats," says the second guy, moving his mouth around the pipe stem.

"Rats?" Arman asks, raising his eyebrows.

"In 1812," Sean says quickly. "Not now." He says it like he wants the reenactors to know he already knew about the straw.

"Military camps have always had trouble with rats and disease," the moustache guy says. It's hard to tell if he's just talking about the past.

The guy with the pipe stretches his legs out and leans back, looking up at the blue sky.

"Nice weather for a battle," he says.

I remember Major Helston saying it rained for days leading up to the siege in 1814.

"Are you boys fighting on our side tomorrow?" moustache guy asks.

"Most of us," Sean tells him. I'm not sure if I should admit I'll be fighting with the Americans. For all I know, they'll jump up and take me prisoner.

We say goodbye, and moustache man raises his tin mug in a toast.

"To King George," he says.

We play along and mumble some kind of agreement.

"Good luck in the battle," Sean adds as we walk away.

"Don't get caught on the north bastion," the pipe guy calls after us. Luckily, thanks to Nicola, we know he's talking about the explosion.

"Right," we call back, grinning.

We continue walking, trying to stay out of the way of the people carrying in supplies and setting up tents. There are a few women wearing 1812-style long dresses and hats mixed in with the soldiers. Every once in a while, people greet each other with hugs like it's a reunion.

At the end of the first row of tents, there's a round tent that looks like it's made out of animal skins. A group of First Nations guys stands in front of it, talking and laughing. They wear leather moccasins and what seems to be a mix of Native and European clothing. One has a heavy battle club tucked into the back of a sash around his waist. He has black war paint on the bottom half of his face. His head is mostly bald, with a tail of black hair sticking up from the top. Another guy wears breeches and a military-style coat with a blue blanket over one shoulder. He has a red turban-like hat decorated with a large white feather. His brown face is handsome and hard-edged.

"I wonder if he's supposed to be Chief John Norton," Sean says. "He led the First Nations warriors at the Siege of Fort Erie."

The face of another First Nations warrior is painted half red and half black. He has feathers hanging from the top of his head and a metal ring in his nose. He notices us watching and glowers, holding up a dangerous-looking battle ax, as if he wants to throw it at us. I can feel Sean tense beside me, and I can imagine how the American soldiers must have been terrified to meet the First Nations warriors in battle.

The guy drops his ax and grins. Then he pulls a cell phone from his waistband and holds it out to me.

"Do you mind taking a picture of us?" he asks.

I hold the cell phone in position while the men squeeze closer. A couple of them pose menacingly, while the others laugh.

"Don't let Major Helston see your phone," I tell the guy as I hand it back. He must know who I'm talking about, because he nods and laughs.

We walk to the end of the Canadian camp and then head back.

"I don't see any black dudes," Arman says, scanning the camp. I cringe, hoping he doesn't sound racist. "Wasn't there supposed to be a unit of ex-slaves?"

"It was called the Coloured Corps," Sean says. "Major Helston said they were stationed at Fort Mississauga during the Siege of Fort Erie, so the unit didn't fight here. But there might have been some black soldiers in the battle."

As we walk back to our camp, we see a crew cab pickup truck pull into the parking area towing a field cannon on a trailer. Another truck pulls in with a horse trailer. Things might get interesting around here tomorrow.

Chapter Thirteen

After dark that night, the field around the fort is dotted with lantern lights. Laughter and music drift on the air. There is no modern music, only rowdy singing to something that sounds like a flute. I can hear the voices of men toasting King George long after Sean and I are in our sleeping bags.

The next morning we have drill practice as usual. The real reenactors drill too.

"It's all about muscle memory," Helston tells us. "You don't want to hesitate when you're in the middle of musket and cannon fire. And you don't want to get tangled up with the next soldier's ramrod or bayonet." Having seen the bayonets and our clumsiness, I have to agree with him.

After drill, we all head down to the river bank. Two American boats are coming across from Buffalo. They'll join the US soldiers already here and attack the fort. Then, once the Americans have taken over, we'll reenact the British-Canadian attack on them. Two months of the war in one day.

The reenactor boats make their way across the river at a diagonal. They started from a spot west of Buffalo and row with the current toward us. I can see the men at the oars, wearing the blue uniform coats of the US regulars and tall black shako hats. The guy in the front of the first boat must be a general, because he's wearing one of those big two-sided hats with a rounded top. None of the men are wearing life jackets, and I remember what Sean said about the reenactors hiding their life jackets under the seats.

The boats slide onto the beach beside our two boats. By now, there is a big crowd of tourists and local people watching from the park in front of the fort and from other boats on the river. I scan the crowd for Nicola, and catch sight of Major Helston instead. He's standing off to the side talking with a man wearing jeans and a zippered gray hoodie. There's something about the way the guy stands that looks tense, and his eyes are hidden behind dark sunglasses. He's obviously not a reenactor, and I wonder what they're talking about. They look out at the river, as if watching for something. Then they nod, without smiling, and move apart. Weird.

Sean nudges me, and I turn back to the action. We watch as the American soldiers march on the fort, and the British surrender. Then we return to camp. We wander through the merchant area, where people in 1812 costume are selling reenactment clothing, muskets, swords, coins, and other stuff. A burly guy dressed as a fur trader has a display of animal furs and piles of blankets and other things they used to trade for furs. At another stall, a guy wears an apron that looks like it's streaked with blood. On a table in front of him are small saws, knives and a few other bizarre-looking tools. There are red splotches on the table cloth, and a sign that says *Surgeon*. Great. He's an 1812 doctor.

ground as if he's been shot. My
umps. I feel like I just had a close
As we advance, I step over other
lying on the ground. I think back
y first day at camp when I couldn't
my musket to fire. My hands shake
first time I reload, but I keep firing,
oading and marching forward.

We get the command to break our
ne into two wings. The British march
n between, and we catch them in
neavy crossfire. The battle ends. The
Americans win, and I'm still standing.

There's a break as we regroup to
fight the Battle of Lundy's Lane, which
took place at the town of Niagara Falls.
I collapse on the ground in some shade
and guzzle water from my musty-smelling
canteen. For a second, I consider deserting
and going to look for Nicola. But as we get
back on our feet and reload our muskets,
a wave of excitement moves through the
reenactors and pulls me with it.

"What's that for?" Arman asks,
pointing at a hacksaw in the middle of
the table.

"Amputation," says the guy with the
bloody apron. "If a soldier has a bad leg
or arm injury, I cut it off."

"Dude!" Armon takes a step back
from the table, looking disgusted.

"No time for fancy stitching," the
doctor adds cheerfully. "If a soldier
survives the amputation, he has a good
chance of living. If I don't cut off the
injured arm or leg, he'll die of blood
infection or gangrene, for sure."

Arman looks a little green himself.
We head back to the mess tent to find
some water. I see Nicola getting lunch
ready with her mom, but we don't get a
chance to talk.

After lunch, Major Helston hands
out red and blue uniform jackets, and we
join the real reenactors. By now, there
are hundreds of them, and hundreds

more people just here to watch. Two British soldiers on horseback pick their way through the crowd. The battlefield is roped off with orange tape. The two armies set up on opposite ends of the field, pulling cannons into position. The audience gathers behind the tape. Several reenactors about our age march, beating drums. Others play something called a fife, which looks like a small flute. They are the Fife and Drum Corps. It's hard to believe young guys like them stood in the middle of the fighting, using their musical instruments to pass on commands.

"Welcome to the annual reenactment at Old Fort Erie," calls out an announcer over loudspeakers. *"The largest War of 1812 reenactment event in Canada."*

I line up with the blue-coated soldiers and stare across the field at the red coats in the distance. This afternoon we're reenacting the Battle of Chippawa

and the Battle o
tonight, we do the

"The Americans
July 3, 1814," the ann
began advancing north
River. They met British
allies at Chippawa Creek

Boom! A cannon bl
battle. Smoke billows acro

Shoulder to shoulder w
soldiers, I march into the s
heart pounds, and my hands a
as I grip my musket. I know
real battle, but I don't want to sc

"Present arms! Fire!" I he
commands through the cracks of m
fire. I stop, raise my gun and fire.

Bang! Bang! Muskets fire on b
sides of me. Gunpowder irritates m
eyes and nose. I can't see what I'm
shooting at through the smoke. I hear
the *crack crack* of answering gunfire.
The man beside me cries out and falls

"The Battle of Lundy's Lane took place July 25, 1814," the announcer begins. *"It was one of the deadliest battles of the war."*

Once again, the cannons blast, and we march across the field. When the battle ends, I break away from the American reenactors and head to the mess tent. As I squeeze through the crowd, I glimpse a man wearing dark sunglasses and a gray hoodie—the guy I saw Helston talking with earlier. He looks out of place among the people dressed like they just stepped out of the past. He stands off to the side, where he has a view of everybody passing by. I walk past, careful not to meet his eyes.

At the mess tent, everyone is talking and laughing. I forget about the guy with the sunglasses and look for Sean.

"That was so cool!" Sean says as we find each other. I grin back at him.

"It will be even better tonight," he promises.

Chapter Fourteen

For the final battle, we move from the field to the fort. The sun is low in the sky as I take my position with the other American soldiers inside the fort. From the wall above the south-west bastion, I watch the red-coated British troops and Canadian militia form lines to attack us. The First Nations warriors gather beside them.

"*After nightfall on August 15, 1814*," the announcer's voice tells us, "*the British, under the command of Lieutenant General Drummond, launched a three-pronged attack on the Americans at Fort Erie.*"

A cannon blast starts the attack. Fireworks shriek, mimicking the sound of rockets fired by the British. Muskets fire at us from the field below. I raise my gun above the stone wall and fire back.

As the British and Canadian troops advance toward us, I try to make out Sean, Arman or Carter through the smoke. But it's getting darker and it's hard to see anything except the flash of musket fire. We blast at the attackers with our muskets and cannons. Then, suddenly, eerie *whoops* rise through the summer air as the First Nations warriors run forward to support the British soldiers.

Now there are soldiers directly below us. They lift ladders into place against the fort wall and begin to climb up. In seconds, they will be on us. Of course, if it was really 1814, we'd be doing our best to shoot them off. I look over the wall and see one guy fall from a lower rung of a ladder. I'm not sure if it's a fake fall or a real fall. I twist around just in time to see the first British soldier come over the wall. Then another. I hesitate, not sure what I'm supposed to do now. A red coat lunges toward me, thrusting a bayonet.

"Hey!" I protest, jumping out of the way. This fight might be phony, but those bayonets could do real damage.

"Sorry," the guy apologizes. "Lost my balance a bit there."

There's something familiar about his voice. Then he grins, and I recognize the man with the pipe we talked to at the British camp earlier. He moves past me, firing his musket at the soldiers behind me.

"Hey!" says an even more familiar voice near my ear. I turn just as Nicola grabs my sleeve and pulls me down against the wall.

"What are you doing here?" I ask as I crouch next to her.

"I'm nursing the wounded," she says. "There were women acting as nurses right in the middle of the battle. And you look like you just got stabbed with a bayonet."

"Yeah. Almost for real," I say.

"Look that way," she tells me, pointing past the barracks to the north bastion. "They're going to blow it up any second."

I barely have time to look.

Boom!

The explosion is louder than I expected. Yellow-orange flames shoot up into the night sky. The soldiers and the people watching from the field gasp and then cheer. I close my eyes and still see the flash of light burned onto the back of my eyelids. My ears ring.

The flames die away, and smoke billows across the fort. As my eyes return to normal, I see bodies littering the ground below the north bastion. My heart jolts, and for a second I wonder if they're really dead. Maybe something went wrong with the fireworks.

"Just think," Nicola says, "two hundred years ago, that was real. Three hundred men died in the explosion, and more in the rest of the fighting."

We stare into the smoke for moment, not saying anything. I think back to earlier in the week when we laughed about the headless ghost and the handless ghost. It doesn't seem funny anymore.

A voice from a loudspeaker cuts into our thoughts. But this time, it's not the reenactment announcer. It seems to be coming from the river. Nicola and I stand up and look over the wall.

"*This is the border patrol*," a deep, amplified voice calls. "*Please stop your engine and prepare to be boarded.*"

Everyone—including the guys playing dead a second ago—rushes to the wall to see what's going on. The river is black but dotted with the lights of boats viewing the reenactment fireworks. The border-patrol boat is obvious by the big beam of light coming from it. It closes in on a small boat caught in the light. It's hard to tell whether the other boat is on the Canadian side of the river or the American.

I expect the border patrol boat to pull up alongside the other boat. But suddenly, the other boat picks up speed. It's making a run for it. The roar of the motors drifts up to the fort as we watch the chase. For a moment, it looks as if the fleeing boat might get away. But the border patrol boat closes in.

"Did they get them?" I jump at the sound of Major Helston's voice, as he steps up beside Nicola. On his other side is a man I almost don't recognize without his dark sunglasses. He's still dressed in jeans and gray hoodie. What is he doing in the middle of the reenactment?

Chapter Fifteen

The guy with the hoodie pulls something out from under his jacket. For a second, I think it might be a handgun. But it's a walkie-talkie. There's the crackle of static.

"The suspects have been apprehended," says a voice from the walkie-talkie. *"Officers are searching the boat."*

The man walks away from us, speaking into the walkie-talkie.

"Dad, what's going on?" Nicola asks.

"The police got a tip that something was going to be smuggled across the river today during the reenactment," Helston tells us. He gestures to the man in the hoodie. "Sergeant Melino is a plainclothes police officer working with the border patrol."

Sergeant Melino makes his way back to us.

"The boat was clean," he says, shaking his head. "It must have been a diversion."

"Does that mean the smugglers made it across?" Helston asks.

"There's a chance they did," the officer says. "We'll keep up a patrol along the shore tonight. If you see anything out of the ordinary, call me."

"Of course," Helston tells him.

I wonder what was being smuggled.

"Thanks for your help, Bruce," the officer says, holding out his hand to shake Helston's.

Bruce? That's Hell Storm's first name? And he's helping the police? This whole thing is weird.

As the reenactment comes to a close, Nicola and I go to search out Sean and the others. We leave through the front gate of the fort, passing reenactors and tourists on their way in for a special lantern tour of the fort. I notice the dark shape of someone walking up from the river. As he steps into the light near the front gate, I see that it's Lieutenant Gunner.

"So, you survived the battle," he says when he sees us.

"Did you meet up with your girlfriend?" I ask, remembering what he said the night we caught him talking on his cell phone.

"Who?"

"I thought you were meeting your girlfriend Saturday night," I say.

"Oh, right," Gunner says, with a laugh. "I guess she stood me up."

The three of us walk back toward the camp. We bump into Sean, Arman and Carter before we get there.

"What did you think?" Sean asks. "Wasn't it cool?"

"Did you see the boat chase?" Arman demands.

Gunner laughs.

"Well, I'll leave you guys to it," he says. "Watch out for the headless ghost."

We laugh and wave goodnight.

"I'm not kidding," he says as he walks off in the direction of his tent. "You should stay in your tents tonight."

Is he serious? I meet Nicola's eyes, and she shrugs as if she's read my mind.

"I guess if there are any ghosts, they would be restless tonight," Carter suggests.

"He's just kidding," Sean says.

"Well, I'm not going to be wandering around tonight after everyone's in bed," Arman says.

A wave of voices and laughter rolls from the camps.

"It doesn't sound like anyone's going to bed for a while yet," I say. "Should we check it out?"

We walk toward the noise, and Nicola takes hold of my arm, tugging me to slow down. We drop a few steps behind the others.

"Did you think that was weird?" she asks, her voice lowered so the others don't hear.

"What? The way Gunner tried to scare us?"

"Yeah," she says. "And what about his girlfriend? It was like he didn't know what you were talking about."

"So?" I say. But puzzle pieces have started shifting around in my head.

Gunner arranging to meet someone on Saturday. I think back to his exact wording. *Right*, he'd said. *Saturday it is*. What if he hadn't been making plans to meet a girlfriend? What if he'd been making plans for something else?

"Are you thinking what I'm thinking?" I ask Nicola.

"That depends," she says. "You don't think Gunner could be involved with smuggling, do you?"

"Nah," I say. "He's a good guy."

But is he? If he wasn't meeting his girlfriend, what was he doing down by the river? Checking that the boats were okay? I picture the boats lying on the shore. Our two boats, and the two American boats. The boats that crossed the river.

Hidden in plain sight. Isn't that what Gunner told us about the British boats that snuck up on the three American schooners? What if something was hidden in the boats? The reenactors who rowed across might not even have known it was there. Gunner could be waiting for the commotion to die down before he moves the stuff.

"I think I know where the smuggled stuff is hidden," I say.

"What are you talking about?" Sean demands. I turn around to see Sean, Arman and Carter staring at us. I hadn't noticed them stop walking.

I meet Nicola's eyes, and she nods for me to go ahead and tell them.

"This might sound crazy," I say. "But we need to go to the river."

Chapter Sixteen

"You've got to tell the police," Sean says after Nicola and I explain everything.

"They're not going to believe us," I say. "We're just guessing."

"Then why not wait until the morning to check the boats?" Sean asks.

"He'll have the stuff moved by then," I point out.

"If there is anything," Nicola says. "We could be totally wrong."

"But you could be right," Arman says.

We decide on a three-pronged attack. Sean and I will go down to the river, Arman and Carter will stand at the edge of the field and keep watch for Gunner, and Nicola will go to the southwest bastion and watch for our signal.

"What's the signal?" Nicola asks.

I think for a second, wishing we had our cell phones. Then I hold up my musket.

"If we find something, I'll fire off a shot."

"But won't that alert Gunner?" Sean says. "The police won't be able to prove he's connected unless they catch him in action, right?"

"Good point," I tell Sean. Sometimes he surprises me.

Nicola reaches into the apron she's wearing over her long dress and pulls out a small flashlight.

"Whoa!" Arman says. "That doesn't look very 1812."

"It's for emergencies," she explains as she hands it to Sean. "You guys take it. You can flash it on and off to signal me."

"Good idea," I tell her. For a second I feel pissed that she gave the flashlight to Sean, not to me, but feeling jealous right now is stupid.

Sean tucks the flashlight into his waistband, and we head toward the river. I look back once and see Nicola disappear through the front gate of the fort. There is no sign of Arman and Carter, but a shadowy tree at the edge of the field seems like a likely hiding spot.

The lights of Buffalo shine on the other side of the river, but on our side, it's dark. I shine the flashlight across the white hulls of the four boats.

"I don't see anything," Sean says.

I move ahead of him to the first boat. I reach under the closest seat and pull out a canvas bag.

"That's just a life jacket," Sean says.

"Give me some light," I tell him.

He directs the flashlight beam on the bag, and we hold our breath as I pull out a bulky shape.

It's a life jacket.

"Frack!"

I reach for the next bag. It's another life jacket. We check the next boat. More life jackets. I kick the side of the boat and swear. I must have got it wrong.

"Maybe there's something inside the life jackets," Sean suggests. He hands me the flashlight and grabs one of the life jackets. He turns it around in his hands, looking for a loose seam.

"I wish I had my Swiss Army knife," he complains.

"Or a bayonet," I say. I look back up at the fort as he fiddles with the life jacket. The walls are dark, and I can't tell if anyone's looking over the bastion wall.

"Got it!" Sean holds up a block of something wrapped tightly in plastic. I don't know what it is exactly, but it doesn't look like it would keep anyone afloat if they needed to use the life jacket. And I'm pretty sure it's not cheese.

Gravel crunches behind us, and we spin around.

"You weren't supposed to see that," says Gunner. He puts a hand up to shield his eyes as I shine the flashlight on him. He doesn't look mad, or even dangerous. If anything, he looks disappointed. Then he smiles in his usual friendly way, and I wonder again if I could be mistaken. But the stuff is in the life jackets, and he's just admitted he knew it was there.

I shift the flashlight to point the beam at the fort. But before I can switch it on and off to signal Nicola, Gunner springs forward and knocks it from my hand.

"You don't need to do that," he says. His voice is calm and still friendly, but it doesn't match what he just did. My heart pounds. I glance over at Sean and see his eyes move to the musket he set down against the boat earlier. Even if he can grab it, I know it's not loaded. We have no way of signaling for help.

"Well," Gunner says, smiling again. "Since you're here, you might as well help me get these to my truck."

I move to stand next to Sean, looking past Gunner to the fort. Maybe we can make a run for it.

"I don't think so," Gunner says, as if answering my thought. He holds up his own musket, pointed right at us. "You can take a chance that there's no real shot in here," he warns. "But I wouldn't, if I were you."

"You won't shoot us," Sean says. His voice sounds calm. I'm impressed.

"I don't *want* to shoot you," Gunner says coolly. "But I will."

Suddenly, light shines on us.

"Police!" calls a deep voice from behind Gunner. "Drop the gun!"

Slowly, Gunner lowers the musket. Sean and I both let out a sigh of relief.

Major Helston, Nicola, Arman and Carter rush up behind Sergeant Melino.

"Are you okay?" Nicola cries, out of breath. Sergeant Melino handcuffs Gunner's hands behind his back, and Nicola steps around them to hug Sean and me.

"How did you know to get help?" I ask Nicola. "We didn't signal you."

She glances over her shoulder at Arman and Carter as they join us.

"We saw Gunner go to his truck," Carter explains. "And we figured he was going to drive it to the river."

I look up the bank and see a dark pickup truck parked on the side of the access road. Sergeant Melino's unmarked SUV sits beside it, the headlights pointed down at us.

Suddenly, my legs feel like jelly as it hits me. We just caught a drug smuggler.

Chapter Seventeen

Sunday morning, there is a memorial service to honor the soldiers who died during the War of 1812. After lunch, there's one final battle reenactment called *The Sortie*, in which American troops march out of the fort and attack the British, breaking their siege. The British retreat, and the Americans keep the fort—at least for a while. The whole war ends a few months later, and the American troops go back to their side of the border. There was no real winner or loser.

After the battle, we return to our tents to pack up. Reenactor camp is over.

We gather inside the fort to hand in our muskets and uniforms. Nicola helps Major Helston return cell phones and other personal items. I look around at the stone walls of the fort. A week ago, I didn't want to be here. Now, I'm sorry to leave. Well, not totally.

My cell phone beeps in my hand as a message comes through. I glance down and see that it's from my mom. There are two more waiting to be read. But for now, I put off reading the texts.

"What's your number?" Nicola asks, holding up her phone. "I'll text you, so you'll have mine."

I grin. In the real 1800s, we'd have to write each other letters with paper and quill pens, and they'd take days or even weeks to get delivered. Now she is only a text away. Nicola punches in Sean's number too. Then Arman's and Carter's.

"See you next year?" she says.

"Maybe," I answer.

She hugs each of us, and I don't mind that she's not just hugging me. Then Major Helston steps up beside her. He's still wearing his red coat, breeches and shako.

"I'm not happy about the way you broke the rules," he says, frowning. "You're lucky you didn't get hurt."

Then his dark look lightens and he holds out a hand to shake ours. "But you boys turned out to be fine soldiers."

Sean and I wave at Nicola one last time as we head to the parking lot where Sean's parents are waiting.

"I can't believe it," I say under my breath to Sean. "I think Major Hell Storm almost smiled at us."

Siege

Sometimes it's hard to tell your enemies from your friends through the smoke.

Author's note

This story and its characters are fictional, but the North American War of 1812 really happened. From June 18, 1812, to December 24, 1814, the United States of America was at war with Great Britain and the colonies of Upper and Lower Canada. In the later part of the war, American troops crossed the Niagara River and captured Fort Erie, in what is now the province of Ontario. Many lives were lost when the British and their allies tried to recapture the fort over the next two months.

Today, Old Fort Erie is a museum, where the major battles related to the siege are reenacted each year. As I write this, the fort is preparing to commemorate the bicentennial of the 1814 Siege.

Although the youth reenactment camp and my characters are fictional, I'll imagine Jason, Sean, Arman, Carter and Nicola up on the wall of the fort as the fireworks explode.

I'd like to thank Heather Gorman, manager/curator at Old Fort Erie, and the reenactors who answered my many questions.

Unlike her protagonist, Jacqueline Pearce enjoys learning about history. The author of numerous books for young people, including *Manga Touch* in the Orca Currents series, Jacqueline lives in Burnaby, British Columbia. For more information, visit jacquelinepearce.ca.